*This book belongs to*

..................................................................................

Walt Disney's

# Pluto Pup
## Goes to Sea

Storybook Favourites

**Reader's Digest Young Families**

Walt Disney's

# Pluto Pup
## Goes to Sea

Illustrations by The Walt Disney Studios
Adapted by Yale Gracey
Story by Annie North Bedford

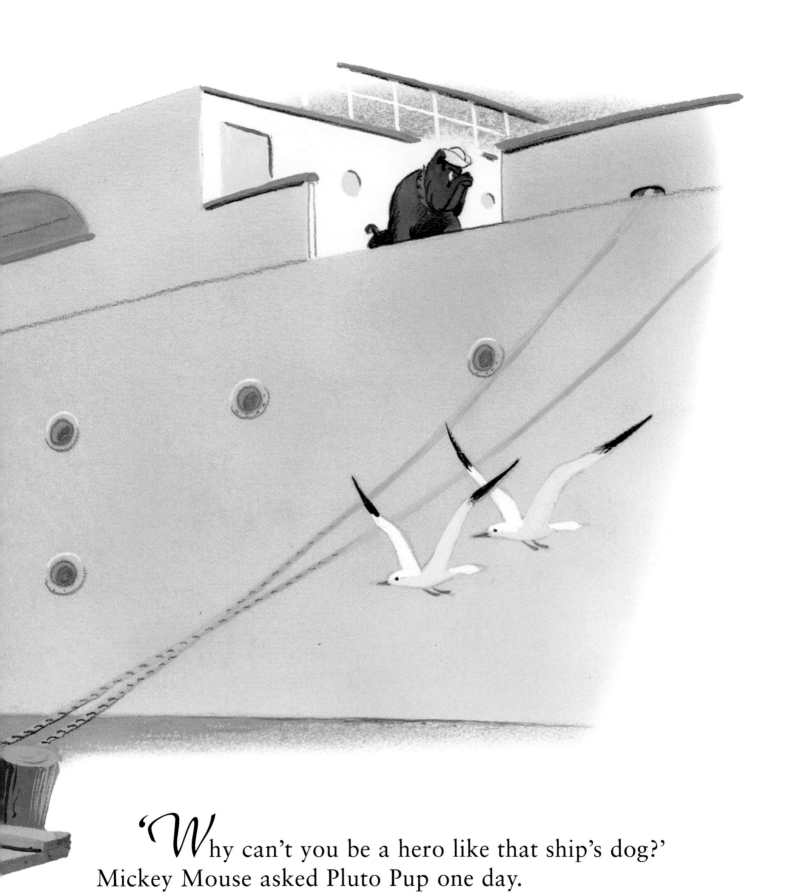

'Why can't you be a hero like that ship's dog?'
Mickey Mouse asked Pluto Pup one day.
They were standing beside an ocean liner, looking up at the deck.

On the deck lay a huge dog, staring proudly out to sea.
'There was a story in the paper about all the lives he's
saved,' said Mickey. 'Why can't you be a dog like that?'

If all you had to do to be a hero was to lie on a deck staring out to sea, Pluto was willing to try it. The next gangplank they came to, up Pluto went.

Mickey did not miss him for a few minutes. Then he whistled and called and looked all around, behind crates and barrels, and in coils of rope. But not a trace of Pluto could he find.

High above, on the deck of a sleek, luxury yacht, Pluto was
sitting all alone, looking proud and haughty, gazing out to sea.

No one on the yacht knew Pluto was on board until they had left the harbour for the open sea. There the waves rose and fell, and the yacht pitched and tossed, and Pluto was as unhappy as a dog can be.

Down below, the sailors shuddered at the dismal moans that came from the deck above. Checking, they soon found the stowaway and led him to a corner of the dark hold, where they made him a bed of old rags.

'Too bad he isn't a smarter mutt,' said the second mate to the first. 'We could use a smart watchdog for the captain's jewels.'

'Sh!' The first mate put a finger to his lips. 'No one must know about those jewels!'

It was too late, though they did not know it. The tough-looking sailor who had found Pluto, was at the top of the hatch and heard what they said.

'Aha! Them jewels will line my pockets soon, and I'll jump ship at the very first port, or my name's not Pegleg Pete!' he growled.

Next day Pluto's nose led him to the lovely food smells in the galley, where the ship's cat lived with the cook.

Pluto heard that catty sizzle, he saw her back arch, and he took off, racing for the deck.

The cat came behind him, moving so fast that as the ship lurched she slid under the rail, down into the sea!

Pluto went over for a better look – and skidded, with a yelp, straight after her!

When the sailors rescued them, they thought Pluto had jumped in to save the cat. They called him a hero. They fussed over him, and the mates moved his bed to the captain's cabin.

'He's just the dog we need to guard the captain's jewels, in spite of his looks,' they said.

Pluto did not like being shut in the cabin, though. He set up such a howl that night that the captain shouted for the mates. 'Take that mutt away. I'd rather be protected from him than by him!' he cried.

So Pluto went back to his first spot on deck, looking proudly out to sea. He kept a sharp eye out for anyone about to fall overboard. He liked the life of a hero.

That was the night Pegleg Pete had picked to steal the captain's jewels. The ship lay close to shore. His friends would meet him with a boat.

So Pete slipped down to the cabin where the captain was asleep, and he hit him with his club and stole the jewels!

With the jewels safely stowed in a small leather pouch, Pegleg Pete signalled to his friends on shore.

When a small light answered, he kicked off his shoe, laid his club beside it, and dived over the rail into the dark waters below.

Splash! He landed and started to swim, but Pluto had heard that splash too.

One of his friends must be overboard! Time to be a hero again!

'Arf! Arf! Arf!' Pluto yelped, and he jumped in too.

'Man overboard!' the lookout yelled. The sailors came running, turned the searchlight on, and soon they picked up Pluto and Pegleg Pete, bobbing in the waters below.

Pete was still sputtering about his cursed luck, and 'that blasted mutt,' but he soon changed his tune. 'I saw the dear mutt slide in,' he claimed, 'and I couldn't bear to think of him drowning, so I jumped in to save him, of course.'

'Is that so?' said the first mate. 'Then what were you doing with the club here beside your shoe?'

'Come to think of it, where's the captain?' the second mate cried. And he ran to the cabin to see.

Pegleg Pete knew then that it was all up with him. 'Let me go!' he cried, and ran for the rail.

But Pluto did not want another bath in that cold water that night! He jumped for Pegleg's trousers and hung on!

Soon the second mate was back, with the captain who had a
big lump on his head where he had been hit by the club.
   'Put Pete in the brig,' the captain said. 'And we'll get you
a medal, sir,' he went on. He was speaking to Pluto Pup!

So when the yacht came home at last, with Pluto sitting proudly up on deck, he wore the biggest, shiniest medal to be had. 'Our Hero' it said in gold.

Mickey was wandering down by the docks, as he did every lonely day, looking for his lost pup, when the yacht came into port.

'Arf!' cried Pluto, when he spied Mickey Mouse.

'Pluto!' cried Mickey. 'Where have you been? And that medal? What does it mean?'

The sailors told Mickey the whole proud tale.

'I guess you won't want to come back home,' Mickey said at the end.

In answer, Pluto gnawed off his medal and laid it at Mickey's feet. He still thought the finest thing of all was to be Mickey Mouse's dog!

*Walt Disney's Pluto Pup Goes to Sea* is a *Disney Storybook Favourites* book

*Walt Disney's Pluto Pup Goes to Sea,* copyright © 1952, 2006 Disney Enterprises, Inc.
Story by Annie North Bedford. Illustrations adapted by Yale Gracey.

This edition was adapted and published in 2009 by
The Reader's Digest Association Limited
11 Westferry Circus, Canary Wharf, London E14 4HE

Editor: Rachel Warren Chadd
Designer: Louise Turpin
Design consultant: Simon Webb

® Reader's Digest, the Pegasus logo and Reader's Digest Young Families
are registered trademarks of
The Reader's Digest Association, Inc.

We are committed both to the quality of our products
and the service we provide to our customers.
We value your comments, so please do contact us on
08705 113366 or via our website at
www.readersdigest.co.uk
If you have any comments or suggestions
about the content of our books, email us at
gbeditorial@readersdigest.co.uk

Printed in China

A Disney Enterprises/Reader's Digest Young Families Book

ISBN 978 0 276 44470 8
Book code 641-029 UP0000-1
Oracle code 504400086H.00.24